The Adventures of Sam Pig

Sam Pig and the
Christmas Pudding
Alison Uttley

Illustrated by Graham Percy

faber and f

LONDON · BC

D0354180

First published in 1941
by Faber and Faber Limited
3 Queen Square London WC1N 3AU
This edition first published in 1989

Phototypeset by
Input Typesetting Ltd, London
Printed in Great Britain by
W. S. Cowell Ltd, Ipswich

A CIP record for this book is available
from the British Library.

ISBN 0–571–15469–7

Sam Pig and the Christmas Pudding

On a distant hill stood the Big House. Although Sam had passed the lodge gates, he had never ventured to go through them. There was a long straight drive between beech trees, and Sam preferred crooked little footpaths. There were many windows twinkling like eyes in the Big House, and a host of chimneys with blue smoke rising from them. Sometimes the hunt met there, and the hounds came down the drive. Sometimes horses with fine coats and grooms at their heads pranced on dainty feet through the gates. It was surely a house of wonders.

Sam asked several friends about it, but only Sally the mare could tell him anything. Sally had taken loads of potatoes to the kitchen door. She knew the names of the horses in the stables, and the grooms and stable boys. She spoke of the fat Irish cook who had given her an apple when she waited at the door.

'Do you think I could go there?' asked Sam wistfully.

'Of course! Don't go prancing about where anyone will see you, that's all. There's a great kitchen garden where you might find a few choice vegetables, and a greenhouse where there are purple grapes, but I shouldn't make too free if I were you.'

'I don't want grapes and vegetables,' said Sam. 'I want to see what the Big House is like. You are an old mare, Sally, and you have travelled, but I've seen nothing much. I only know the pig-cote and stable at the farm, and the Witch's cottage.'

'Do be careful, Sam. Don't do anything rash like going into the house,' warned the mare.

'I'll be careful, Sally,' laughed Sam, but he was quite sure he wanted to go into that great house on the hill.

The next day he set off with his knapsack on his back and his stick in his hand. He took the quiet ways through the fields, and then he scrambled

through the hedge into the road. Before him stood the fine iron gates and the little lodge with its diamond-paned windows. Sam looked admiringly at the lodge. It was just the right size for him and his family, and not much larger than the pig-cote at the farm. He walked boldly through the gates and started up the drive as if he were quite used to a broad gravelled road.

The lodge-keeper's wife was hanging out the washing at the back and she didn't see him. Nobody stopped the little pig who marched boldly towards the great front door. He took one look at the enormous knocker, and the big bell hanging above the portal, and he decided that the back door was more suitable to his height and his small dignity.

He went under the windows round the terrace, trotting softly as a shadow, in and out of the bands of sunlight which fell on the pathway. A glass door stood open, and Sam Pig peered round the corner into the room. There were crowds of books on the walls, red books, blue and brown ones.

'More books than the leaves of the forest,' thought Sam.

He padded across the carpet which was soft as the moss in the woodland, and he stared in wonder at the fairytales which pushed each other on the shelves. He took down a book, but there were no

pictures, and he couldn't understand a word. Then he noticed the writing-table with its sheets of snowy paper, its pens and large brass inkstand.

'Ah!' cried Sam with a little squeal of joy. 'I've always wanted to write in something more lasting than mud or water.'

He dipped his small foot in the ink and made a print on the clean white paper.

'Sam Pig. His mark,' said Sam, solemnly. He admired it for a minute or two, and he blotted it with a nice new piece of blotting-paper as pink as his own tongue. He felt very proud of himself, and he went quietly out of the glass door.

Round the corner were the stables, and Sam heard the whistle of the grooms and the hissing as they fettled the horses. He didn't stop to talk to them, he went to the back door. It stood wide open, inviting all to enter. He passed along a stone-paved passage to the kitchen. He stayed at the door peering through a crack at all he could see. Servants were working at the great table in the centre of the room, and a blazing fire crackled on the hearth. Sam felt at home at once, and he sniffed the good smells and stared at the winking copper pans and dishes. They were big enough for baths, he thought, rather nervously.

Then the two little kitchen-maids spoke, and Sam pricked up his ears.

'Why do we have to make Christmas pudding now, cook?' asked one of the girls.

'Yes. Why do we make it so early?' asked the other.

'Shure, the longer it's made, the foiner 'twill be,' replied the cook, and at the sound of her voice with its deep rich tones Sam took a step nearer.

''Tis as grand intoirely as Leary O'Gorman's puddin', as took to its heels and made off with the hounds after it! Indade, it is! Now cut them raisins,

and give me the currants and beat me some eggs, and mince the apples, and grind the almonds and bring me the sup of spirits to add to it. Glory be, this'll be a grand puddin', it will.'

The two little kitchen-maids shook their white-capped heads, and tossed their blue skirts and ran here and there to do the bidding of the stout good-natured cook. Sam liked the cook very much. He admired her fat rosy face, and her stout red arms, and her twinkling eyes. He waited till the two kitchen-maids had gone to the pantry and the cook's back was turned. Then he tiptoed, soft as a mouse, across the stone floor. He disappeared under the wide table in a flash, and there he sat. The table was a roof over Sam's head, and the little pig felt that he could live there for ever, listening to the talk,

eating the scraps which fell, smelling the fragrant odours of rich cooking.

'Tell us about that pudding of Leary O'Gorman's, dear cook,' wheedled one of the kitchenmaids.

'Yes, do, darling cook,' said the other girl.

'That puddin' as walked? It was a long time ago in Old Ireland. I heard tell of it, when I was a bit of a child no bigger nor a quart jug.'

The kitchen-maids laughed and Sam chuckled under the table.

'It was a little leprechaun that fell into the puddin' and got put in the pot by mistake. All stirred up in the puddin' he was, and nobody any the wiser. When they put the pot on the fire, he let out a screech as you could have heard from here to Killarney, and out he lepped and was off, and he inside the pudding for sure, so as everybody thought that puddin' was bewitched intoirely.'

'What happened then?' asked the maids, breathlessly.

'Oh, he lepped out of the kitchen, and over the door, and away he went, and the whole lot of 'em after him. Horses and hounds and huntsmen, all went in full cry after that bouncing puddin'.'

'And did they catch him?'

'No, and they didna! They're running yet, so they say. They're legging it up mountains and over lakes and through the bogs of Old Ireland, for never a one of 'em can lay hold of the little fellow in Leary O'Gorman's puddin'.'

'We like that story,' smiled the little maids. 'Tell us another, cook.'

'Arrah, whisht! We must get this monstrous pudding in the pot. Now fetch me the magics for it. It's on the dresser they are, this minute. A silver horseshoe for luck, and may I be the one as gets it.

A silver button for a bachelor. A silver thimble for an old maid, God bless her. A silver ass for some fool, and I knows who that is. A silver wishbone, a ring for marriage, and a silver baby for a new-born child.'

The girls laughed and dropped the charms into the pudding. Sam's eyes nearly popped out of his head. What a pudding it must be to have a donkey in it, and a baby as well as smaller things like Sally's horseshoe! He tried to get a peep, but there was no chance. The three servants were standing close to the table, and he could only sniff and sniff at the delicious smells above his head.

'Now stir it about for luck the two of you, and wish a wish, and it'll be afther coming true,' commanded the cook.

There was much laughter and teasing as the big pudding-spoon was scraped round the bowl and Sam nearly split his buttons off with excitement.

'Shure now,' said the cook. 'You've wished your wishes and I've wished mine, glory be. Now for a sup of brandy to keep it for years if so be the misthress wants it. You girls go to the dairy for eggs, for I'll drop two or three more in it. Take the can and skimmer with you, and bring some cream.'

When the two girls had gone down the stone passage, Sam Pig came out from under the table, intent on looking at the silver ass, the baby, the

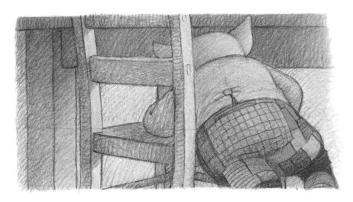

wishbone and all the things in the magical pudding. The cook had taken her newspaper to the fire for a minute's peace, and there she sat with never a thought that a little pig was creeping about the room behind her.

Sam climbed on a chair and leaned over the great bowl where the pudding lay. He was stooping low, tasting the mixture, when the girls came trotting along with their wooden heels clacking on the stones. The cook rustled her paper and folded it up. Sam started, overturned, and toppled into the bowl.

He struggled wildly, and in a moment he was smothered in currants and flour and all the sweet things of the pudding.

'Here are the eggs and cream, cook,' said the maids, tripping lightly across the floor.

'Beat 'em up for me. I'm tired, and I must get this puddin' in the pot. It's a monstrous puddin', and it has taken all the blessed morning to make it.'

She poured the eggs over Sam's floury ears, and gave a few beats with her wooden spoon on Sam's little hard head. He kept very quiet, and ate a few almonds and raisins, so it wasn't too bad.

'When she puts me in the pot I shall find all those magics she talked about. They are somewhere in the pudding, but I can't lay my hands on them yet. When I'm ready I shall take a leap like that fairy man and run off.'

So Sam made himself comfortable in the big round bowl.

The cook tied a cloth round the pudding and lowered it into an iron pan over the fire.

'Faith! It's a heavy puddin' it is!' she remarked. 'It seems to be bigger than I thought it was. It's surely the grandest I've ever made!'

Sam bobbed about in the water, and suddenly he felt the heat of it. He didn't wait any longer. He gave a loud shriek and leapt out of the pan and back again, bouncing over the fire.

The girls gave a cry as they saw the pudding rise and fall. Surely the pudding was bewitched! It gave another jump, and this time it leapt right out of the pan. It dropped with a thud on the floor and rolled towards the door. Sam's little legs were paddling as hard as they could, under the cloth, and Sam rolled and bounced and spun like a top as he went over the stones.

'Hi! Stop! The pudding's running away! It's racing like mad! Stop it! It's our Christmas pudding!' called the little kitchen-maids, scampering after Sam.

'Bedad! It *must* be a leprechaun as is in it,' moaned the cook, with her hand on her heart. 'If we can lay hold on him he will be obliged to give us anything we ask for – a purse of gold, a carriage and pair, a diamond ring – '

'No!' squealed Sam. 'No! I haven't got anything at all.' He rolled and stumbled through the door and then he got his little legs free, and he took to his heels.

'It's not a fairy man. It sounds like a little pig,' said one of the maids.

'After it! After it!' cried the other, throwing her shoe at Sam.

'Fairy leprechauns often squeal like pigs,' said the cook, hurrying after them, 'The little people mostly squeal like piglings. Begorra! It must be a leprechaun as tumbled in the puddin' with those charms we put in. Never again will I mix a magic in a puddin'.'

But away raced Sam, across the wide stone yard. The groom came from the stable and tossed a bucket of water after the tumbling rolling pudding. He called the dogs, but they recognized Sam's voice and they just laughed.

'Another trick of little Sam Pig's,' they barked, and they lay on their backs with joy.

Down the drive scuttled Sam Pig, with the pudding-cloth round his head and body, and his four little trotters paddling over the ground. After him came the red-faced cook, the two kitchen-maids, the groom, and the gardener, the dairy-maid and the gardener's boy. They ran and they ran, but they couldn't catch Sam. The lodge-keeper came hurrying out to see what was the matter. He stretched out a hand to stop the runaway pudding, but Sam slipped between his legs and the man fell sprawling.

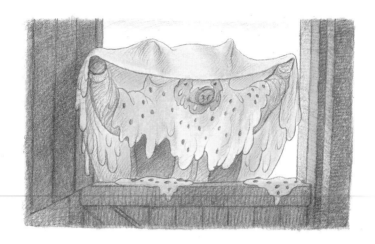

Away went Sam, through the hedge, and into the fields. He left his pursuers far behind, and at last, weary, but not at all hungry – for he had been nibbling the currants and rich spiced pudding – he reached home.

'Sam! Oh Sam! Is it you?' cried Sister Ann, when the little pig opened the door and rushed in with his pudding-cloth waving like a torn flag.

'I'm a Christmas pudding, come to bring you all magical presents,' laughed Sam.

'Sam! Where have you been?' asked Bill and Tom, staring at their brown-and-white brother, encased in a big pudding.

Old Brock shook his head and waited for Sam to explain.

'I've been inside the Big House, and I got mixed up with the Christmas pudding, Brock,' said Sam. 'I've brought you the charms the Irish cook put into it. She thought I was a leprechaun, when I leaped out of the pot and made off!'

Sam hunted in his pockets and brought out the treasures. A silver button for Brock, for he was the bachelor. A silver wishbone for Tom. A silver horseshoe for Sally the mare. A silver ring for Bill. A thimble and a baby for Ann.

'I'll keep the little silver donkey for myself,' said Sam. 'I thought they were putting a real donkey in the pudding, and the only real animal who got in was me!'